Celebrity Quiz-o-rama™
POP PARTY
Pop Quizzes, Party Ideas, and More!

Celebrity Quiz-o-rama™

Celebrity ?uiz-o-rama™
POP PARTY
Pop Quizzes, Party Ideas, and More!

by Jo Hurley

SCHOLASTIC INC.

New York   Toronto   London   Auckland   Sydney   Mexico City   New Delhi   Hong Kong

No part of this work may be reproduced, stored in a retrieval system, or transmitted in any form or by any means, electronic, mechanical, photocopying, recording, or otherwise, without written permission of the publisher. For information regarding permission, write to Scholastic Inc., Attention: Permissions Department, 555 Broadway, New York, NY 10012.

ISBN 0-439-24408-0

12 11 10 9 8 7 6 5 4   0 1 2 3 4 5 6/0

Printed in the U.S.A.
First Scholastic printing, October 2000
Design: Peter Koblish

??? TABLE OF ??? CONTENTS

Celebrity Quiz-o-rama™
POP PARTY
Pop Quizzes, Party Ideas, and More!

INTRODUCTION
Welcome to the Fun House

The party's started . . .

You've made enough popcorn to go around . . .

Your BFFs have arrived . . .

But the MOST important question is still up in the air.

Who knows the most about music, movie, and TV superstars?

Is it you? Your best friend? Your other best friend?

You need a pop party to find out for sure. This awesome party book is packed with laughs, trivia, and activities guaranteed to set your head spinning . . . but in a good way!

Make that times two! This party primer is two books in one:

You get:

• *fifteen fun "pop" quizzes based on your favorite singing and acting superstars!*

• *ten party games and activities to keep you busy, busy, busy—until you're too pooped to pop!*

Plus—there's a super-duper pop party scoring system inside! Every time you and your friends finish a test or play a game, you earn Pop Points. Add 'em up and see your Pop-Q sail off the charts!

Who'll be crowned Pop Party Princess or Prince?

Pop 'til you drop—and find out!

1

?UIZ 1
Funky Hunks & Girly Girls

Oh, no! These stars are *lost*! Identify what bands and shows each boy and girl superstar belongs to . . . before they get lost for good!

1. Frankie Muniz
a) *Roswell*
b) *Friends*
c) *Malcolm in the Middle*

2. Isaac, Taylor, and Zac
a) BBMak
b) Hanson
c) Take Five

3. Devin Lima, Rich Cronin, and Brad Fischetti
a) BBMak
b) No Authority
c) LFO

QUIZ 1

4. Tionne "T-Boz" Watkins, Rozanda "Chili" Thomas, and Lisa "Left Eye" Lopes
a) TLC
b) M2M
c) PYT

5. Leslie Bibb
a) *Roswell*
b) *Popular*
c) *7th Heaven*

6. Marion Raven and Marit Larsen
a) PYT
b) M2M
c) Innosense

7. Majandra Delfino
a) *Roswell*
b) *Dawson's Creek*
c) *Moesha*

8. David Gallagher
a) *7th Heaven*
b) *Malcolm in the Middle*
c) *The Wild Thornberrys*

3

? ? ? Celebrity Quiz-o-rama™ ? ? ?

9.   Nick Lachey, Drew Lachey, Jeff Timmons, and Justin Jeffre
- a)   LFO
- b)   98°
- c)   Take 5

10.   Justin Timberlake, JC Chasez, Joey Fatone, Chris Kirkpatrick, and Lance Bass
- a)   98°
- b)   Backstreet Boys
- c)   'N Sync

11.   Lindsay Armaou, Keavy Lynch, Sinead O'Carroll, and Edele Lynch
- a)   Innosense
- b)   B*witched
- c)   Spice Girls

12.   James Van Der Beek
- a)   *Roswell*
- b)   *7th Heaven*
- c)   *Dawson's Creek*

13.   Shane Filan, Mark Freehily, Kian Eagan, Nicky Byrne, and Bryan McFadden

QUIZ 1

   a)   Westlife
   b)   'N Sync
   c)   Backstreet Boys

14. Justin Berfield

   a)   *Friends*
   b)   *Malcolm in the Middle*
   c)   *7th Heaven*

15. Bubbles

   a)   *The Simpsons*
   b)   *Rugrats*
   c)   *The Powerpuff Girls*

Find the answers to each quiz at the back of the book.

Scorecard

1–6 right: You got the "who's who" blues.
Pop Points: 0
7–12 right: You got the semi-scoop. **Pop Points: 1**
12–14 right: Way to know those pop peeps!
Pop Points: 3
All 15 right: You are *definitely* in the know.
Pop Points: 5

Pop Point Total _____

PARTY GAME

"I Really Love You, but I Just Can't Smile!"

Before you start gabbing about how much you just *loooooove* your favorite hunks, play this goofy game! The more people who play . . . the BETTER!

1. Sit in a circle.

2. One person starts off by turning to the person on his or her left and saying "I love you, I love you, I really really love you, but I just can't smile!" Your goal: Make that person LAUGH.

3. You want to make funny faces and noises to crack them up! Your goal when someone's doin' it to you: stonefaced.

4. The game continues around the circle until everyone laughs.

5. Props are a fun addition to this goofy game: get waxed lips, mustaches, funny glasses, and other items to cause a real laugh riot!

Give yourself a Pop Point for playing!

Pop Point Total _____

¿QUIZ 2
Name's the Same

Do you ever get your pop stars mixed up? Can you sort out each Scott, Josh, and Jessica? See if you can correctly ID the actors and singers in each question below.

1.   This actor plays Pacey on *Dawson's Creek*.
a)   Jonathan Jackson
b)   Josh Hartnett
c)   Joshua Jackson
d)   Jonathan Brandis

2.   He's the cute host of MTV's popular show *Total Request Live*.
a)   Carly Pope
b)   JC Chasez
c)   Tom Green
d)   Carson Daly

? ? ? Celebrity Quiz-o-rama™ ? ? ?

3. He stars in the blockbuster movie *X-Men* and appeared on *Party of Five*, too!

a) James Van Der Beek
b) James Marsden
c) James Taylor
d) Jason Behr

4. This former ballerina now dances with aliens on the TV show *Roswell*.

a) Sarah Polley
b) Sarah Michelle Gellar
c) Sara Rue
d) Shiri Appleby

5. She starred in *Selena*, dated singer Puff Daddy, and had a hit album, *On the 6*.

a) Jennifer Lopez
b) Jessica Simpson
c) Jennifer Love Hewitt
d) Jessica Biel

6. He's best buddies with fellow actor Ben Affleck.

a) Matt Keeslar
b) Gabriel Damon
c) Matt Lillard
d) Matt Damon

QUIZ 2

7.   He plays an out-of-this-world cast member on
3rd Rock from the Sun.
a)   Jonathan Taylor Thomas
b)   Joseph Gordon-Levitt
c)   Joshua Jackson
d)   Justin Timberlake

8.   He's one of the singers for the hot boy band LFO.
a)   Brad Pitt
b)   Brad Rower
c)   Brad Fischetti
d)   Brad Renfro

9.   She's a hot VJ on MTV.
a)   Amanda Peet
b)   Ananda Lewis
c)   Tatyana Ali
d)   Amanda Bynes

10.   He's a new hunk who starred in the show *Young*
Americans **on the WB.**
a)   Scott Foley
b)   Rodney Scott
c)   Scott Speedman
d)   Scott Moffatt

? ? ? Celebrity Quiz-o-rama™ ? ? ?

11. She left *Party of Five* for her own series, *Time of Your Life*.

a) Jenna Elfman

b) Jennie Garth

c) Jennifer Lopez

d) Jennifer Love Hewitt

12. This super singer who uses only one name starred in a scary movie with Jennifer Love Hewitt.

a) Brandy

b) Monica

c) Aaliyah

d) Selena

Scorecard

1–4 right: *No blame* in this name game. G'luck next time! **Pop Points: 0**

5–7 right: *No shame* in this name game. You did OK! **Pop Points: 1**

8–10 right: *You can tame* the name game. **Pop Points: 3**

All 12 right: *Claim to fame?* Nailing the name game! **Pop Points: 10**

Pop Point Total _____

PARTY GAME
Star Search Party

While you remember your pop trivia . . . trade places with stars you love!

As your party guests walk into the house, stick a piece of paper on their backs with tape or a safety pin. Make sure they can't see what's on the paper. What's on it? Ahead of time, you have written down the names of current pop stars. For example, one guest has "Britney Spears" taped to her back; while another guest has "JC Chasez." You can mix in stars from TV and movies as well as music. Sound easy? Not so fast!

The object of this party game is for guests to figure out who they are by asking questions. They can ask anything that can be answered with Yes or No.

Am I a singer?

Am I a boy?

Do I star in movies or television?

Give yourself a Pop Point for playing!

Pop Point Total _____

?UIZ 3

Caught in the Act!

In the sixteen questions below, you need to fill in the blanks with the missing names of actors from movies or TV shows. How many pop stars can you "catch in the act"?

Bonus: Whoever unscrambles these clues the fastest gets one bonus Pop Point!

Huge Hint: Here's the list of names and titles to choose from:

Austin Powers
Ben Savage
Sabrina, the Teenage Witch
Friends
Heath Ledger
Stuart Little

Popular
Ever After
Shiri Appleby
Sarah Michelle Gellar
The Simpsons
Joshua Jackson

QUIZ 3

Tangi Miller   *Malcolm in the Middle*
Leelee Sobieski   Natalie Portman
Men in Black   *Titanic*

1. Seth Green as Scott Evil in _____
2. Will Smith as Agent J in _____
3. _____ as Buffy in *Buffy the Vampire Slayer*
4. Leonardo DiCaprio as Jack Dawson in
_____
5. Frankie Muniz as Malcolm in
_____
6. Jonathan Lipnicki as George Little in
_____
7. _____ as Queen Amidala in *Star Wars: The Phantom Menace*
8. Drew Barrymore as Danielle De Barbarac in
_____
9. _____ as Cory Matthews on *Boy Meets World*
10. The voice of Hank Azaria as Apu and Chief Wiggums in _____
11. Leslie Bibb as Brooke McQueen in _____
12. _____ as Pacey Whitter in *Dawson's Creek*

? ? ? Celebrity Quiz-o-rama™ ? ? ?

13. _____ as Liz Parker in *Roswell*

14. Melissa Joan Hart as Sabrina in _____

15. _____ as Gabriel Martin in *The Patriot*

16. Jennifer Aniston as Rachel Greene in _____

Scorecard

1–6 right: Turn up the tube! **Pop Points: 1**

7–11 right: You've got *a little bit* of character. **Pop Points: 3**

12–15 right: Do you see every movie *twice*? WOW! **Pop Points: 6**

All 16 right: The *point* is: Your knowledge of actors is A+. **Pop Points: 10**

Don't forget the bonus point for the fastest answers!

Pop Point Total _____

PARTY GAME
Slumber Party Screening Room

No pop party would be a smash hit without popcorn and other munchies! Make sure you have plenty of eats and drinks *plus* a VCR filled with movie rentals! Decide ahead of time if you want the party to have a spooky, silly, or romantic theme. Rent *Titanic* and watch it for the tenth time, or turn on the tube TV and find an old movie or musical to watch together. Some favorite flicks just right for you to rent: *Ever After, The Princess Bride, Ten Things I Hate About You, Never Been Kissed,* or *Toy Story* (both 1 *and* 2). Of course, you can always tune into your favorite TV shows, too.

Give yourself a Pop Point for playing!

ǫUIZ 4
Pop Geography

Forget *Beverly Hills, 90210*. The hottest location in the world of pop is . . . the birthplace of your favorite stars! This is one quickie quiz you need to *address* seriously! Can you make the matches?

1. *Boy Meets World* **sweetheart born in Mesa, Arizona.**
a) Jennie Garth
b) Danielle Fishel
c) Calista Flockhart
d) Brandy

2. **Have you ever met an "Angel" from Philadelphia, Pennsylvania?**
a) Ashton Kutcher
b) James Marsden
c) David Boreanaz
d) Nicholas Brendon

QUIZ 4

3.   The actress who plays Joey Potter was not born anywhere near Dawson's Creek. She is a native of Toledo, Ohio!
a)   Michelle Williams
b)   Katie Holmes
c)   Tangi Miller
d)   Alyson Hannigan

4.   You can call this western city and state combo Isaac, Taylor, and Zac Hanson-land . . .
a)   Boston, Massachusetts
b)   Tulsa, Oklahoma
c)   New Orleans, Louisiana
d)   Tallahassee, Florida

5.   This song starlet was "One in a Million" in her hometown of Detroit, Michigan.
a)   Aaliyah
b)   Brandy
c)   Jennifer Love Hewitt
d)   Britney Spears

? ? ? Celebrity Quiz-o-rama™ ? ? ?

6. *7th Heaven* beauty Jessica Biel got "confidence" from being born in a place that sounds pretty brave.
a) New York, New York
b) Santa Fe, New Mexico
c) Nashville, Tennessee
d) Boulder, Colorado

7. No Authority bandmates Tommy, Danny, Eric, and Ricky all come from Los Angeles . . . in what state?
a) Nevada
b) California
c) Washington
d) New Mexico

8. What four-girl band from England is scary, posh, sporty, and other stuff?
a) 702
b) Innosense
c) Destiny's Child
d) Spice Girls

9. It's not likely that this actress who plays Buffy caught monsters in her birthplace of New York City.
a) Sarah Michelle Gellar
b) Selma Blair

c) Keri Russell
d) Aaliyah

10. This actor and his brother Casey come from Cambridge, Massachusetts.
a) Ben Affleck
b) Frankie Muniz
c) James Marsden
d) Fred Savage

11. This *Popular* star comes from over the border . . . Vancouver, Canada!
a) Jennie Garth
b) Carly Pope
c) Keri Russell
d) Alyssa Milano

12. Like, don't have a cow, man! This dude's from Springfield, and Homer says he's in 'toon!
a) Spider-Man
b) Justin Timberlake
c) Bart Simpson
d) Shane West

? ? ? Celebrity Quiz-o-rama™ ? ? ?

Bonus: What actress was born in Winona, Minnesota?

Scorecard

1–4 right: On the road to *nowhere*? **Pop Points: 0**
5–8 right: Destination: middle of the road!
Pop Points: 1
9–11 right: Your Pop-Q potential puts you on the map! **Pop Points: 3**
All 12 right: Will the Pop Geography whiz please stand up? **Pop Points: 6**

   Did you get the bonus right? Add one more Pop Point, partner!

Pop Point Total _____

PARTY GAME
Charting the Stars

Part of pop geography is naming the right place at the right time. This game involves paper and pencils, which you need to hand out to everyone.

Make a chart on paper that looks like this:

	Girl	Guy	Place	Song
P				
O				
P				
M				
U				
S				
I				
C				

Leave blank all of the items that are going to be printed. Notice the 8 letters running down the side as well as the four categories at the top. You can pick any word(s) that relate(s) to the topic. The topic here is POP MUSIC, but you could just as easily pick HIT SHOWS, MOVIES, BOOKS, and PLACES. The categories are up to you!

Your ultimate goal: fill in the grid.

? ? ? Celebrity Quiz-o-rama™ ? ? ?

Here's how: Look at the top category, Guys. Then look over to the first letter, P. Write in the grid box the name of a Guy that starts with the letter P. You'd fill in a girls' name under Girl and so on. Here's an example of a grid with a few of the squares filled in:

	Guy	Girl	Place	Song
P	Puff Daddy	Pink	Philadelphia	
O	O-town		Oklahoma	"Open Your Heart" (Madonna)
P		Madonna	Massachusetts	
M				
U	Usher			"Unpretty" (TLC)
S		Scary Spice		
I			Iceland	"I Want It That Way" (BSB)
C	C-Note			"Crazy" (Britney Spears)

This is where the fun begins. After fifteen minutes or so, have one player start reading answers aloud. If any two people match their response, they must cross off their item. The goal in this game is to pick the most unusual answers. Try to think of answers no one else will find! When you see how many words you have left at the end, count each one as a point for yourself.

Pop Point Total _____

ΩUIZ 5
Totally Un-*pop*-ular

Even pop superstars have bad days! Can you guess which stars had totally un-*pop*-ular experiences? Use your best guesses and then check them against the answers printed at the back of the book.

1.   He says that when he was a kid, his life was mainly about comic books, cartoons, and snowboarding. That was before *he* was all that!
   a)   Ashton Kutcher
   b)   Freddie Prinze, Jr.
   c)   Leonardo DiCaprio
   d)   Lance Bass

2.   This actor heartthrob says he once went up to a girl to ask her out . . . but the girl introduced him to her *boyfriend*. Party of *one*, please!
   a)   Joshua Jackson
   b)   Will Smith

c)   Scott Wolf
d)   James Van Der Beek

3.   A piece of girl's clothing landed on his head during a concert and he missed a few dance steps! Talk about being "out" of sync.
a)   Chris Kirkpatrick
b)   Kevin Richardson
c)   Ricky Martin
d)   Rich Cronin

4.   Ouch! This pop princess skidded across the stage on a frosted cupcake! She didn't wanna do that one more time.
a)   Christina Aguilera
b)   Mandy Moore
c)   Jessica Simpson
d)   Britney Spears

5.   This singer says she blushes easily. It's a good thing that she doesn't turn the color of her 'do!
a)   Jennifer Lopez
b)   Mariah Carey
c)   Christina Aguilera
d)   Pink

QUIZ 5

6. During rehearsals for an awards show, this TV hunk mooned the crowd — and got caught by the camera! He was up a *creek* . . . without a paddle!
a) Jason Behr
b) Bryce Johnson
c) Joshua Jackson
d) Ben Savage

7. Grandma caught this "spoiled" rap starlet kissing a boy in *church*!
a) T-Boz
b) Da Brat
c) Pepa
d) Missy Elliot

8. This pop beauty felt like a genie breaking out of a bottle when she slammed into a glass door by mistake.
a) Britney Spears
b) Christina Aguilera
c) Mandy Moore
d) Jessica Simpson

9. When this diva bleached her hair in seventh grade, it turned bright orange! But she had a "Fantasy" it would get better again — and it did!

a) Christina Aguilera
b) Gwen Stefani
c) Charlotte Church
d) Mariah Carey

10. During an audition, this boy really met world when his pager went off! Like, he didn't get the job, in case you were wondering.

a) Ben Savage
b) Frankie Muniz
c) Ben Affleck
d) Scott Foley

11. During a fight with a boy in fifth grade, this actress had her worst experience here on earth: her retainer flew out of her mouth!

a) Rachael Leigh Cook
b) Leelee Sobieski
c) Mila Kunis
d) Melissa Joan Hart

QUIZ 5

12. *Urp!* This singer's temperature went way over ninety-eight degrees when he upchucked on stage from food poisoning!
a) Rob Thomas
b) Usher
c) Drew Lachey
d) Justin Timberlake

13. This actress probably wanted to scream *two* times when she walked into a tree during a movie shoot!
a) Sarah Michelle Gellar
b) Sarah Polley
c) Jennifer Love Hewitt
d) Neve Campbell

14. After getting a part in an acne commercial as the "after" face (meaning *no* pimples), this actor felt a little "leery." Why? He had a zit attack and had to be smeared with coverup makeup!
a) James Van Der Beek
b) Shane West
c) Scott Speedman
d) Joshua Jackson

? ? ? Celebrity Quiz-o-rama™ ? ? ?

15. This BSB was mortified to see something hanging from his nose during a photo shoot.
a) Rich Cronin
b) Kevin Richardson
c) JC Chasez
d) Taylor Hanson

16. This beautiful actress and singer was having the time of her life onstage . . . when all of a sudden she belched into a microphone!
a) Jennifer Love Hewitt
b) Brandy
c) Carly Pope
d) Britney Spears

17. This sweet-as-candy singer fell head over heels at her school's homecoming — when her shoe's heel split in two!
a) Hoku
b) Mandy Moore
c) Pink
d) Mya

QUIZ 5

18. How did this songstress feel when a seagull pooped all over her legs at the beach? Be careful "where you are"!

a) Mya
b) Vitamin C
c) Jessica Simpson
d) Mandy Moore

Scorecard

1–6 right: OK, so embarrassments aren't your best subject. **Pop Points: 0**

7–13 right: OOPS! A few hits but then you came to a screeching pop *stop*! **Pop Points: 2**

14–17 right: WHEW! You heard about these superstar slip ups! **Pop Points: 5**

All 18 right: You must be soooo POPular!
Pop Points: 10

Pop Point Total _____

?UIZ 6

Food Fight!

Snack time, anyone? These bands are guaranteed to give you the pop party munchies. How fast will it take you to unscramble their names?

1. **"Someday" this band will get even sweeter!**

   USRGA   RYA

   _____   ____

2. **You could have this band on a bagel! Their name really stands for: Living Off Experience.**

   EHT   OXL

   ____   ____

3. **This singer is so good it's "Criminal"! You might want to listen to one of her songs every day . . . to keep the doctor away.**

   NIAOF   LEPAP

   _____   _____

QUIZ 6

4. Serve this singer up with gravy and mashed pota-
toes and he'll do anything for love!

AOEFATML

_____

5. You can sprinkle this rap girl band on all your food
to spice it up.

TALS   AEPP

_____ -N- _____

6. This Irish band will "Linger" in your "Dreams" for
a berry, berry long time! (It's popular around Thanks-
giving time, too.)

HET   NSCRBRIEARE

_____ _____

7. This seasoned British Band had loads of "Girl
Power"!

PIESC   GISRL

_____   _____

8. Singer Evan Dando sings for this band with a sour
name.

EOAHNLDEMS

_____

? ? ? Celebrity Quiz-o-rama™ ? ? ?

9. This soulful singer has a name that sounds like a drink.

RBYAND

_____

10. This may not actually be a food you can eat, but this band has a fishy name: Hootie and the

IWLHOBSF

_____

11. You might eat this band's food name while making a pie in the autumn.

GISAMNSH KNUPISMP

_____   _____

Bonus: You may not eat this, but you'll find it in orange juice.

MIACTVIN

_____   ____

Scorecard

1–3 right: You're *starving* for your basic pop food groups! **Pop Points: 1**

4–7 right: You'll be hungry again in an hour or so. **Pop Points: 2**

8–9 right: You're simply stuffed with superstar know-how! **Pop Points: 3**

All 11 right: You're like a pop star gourmet . . . *perfect*! **Pop Points: 4**

Got the Bonus right? Give yourself a pat on the back and an extra Pop Point.

Pop Point Total _____

*Q*UIZ 7
Music by the Numbers

There are so many bands with numbers in their name! Can you answer fifteen questions about these Number One bands you can *count* on?

1.   Big brother Nick Lachey called his brother Drew and asked him to join this band — even though Drew lived three thousand miles away at the time!

   a)   Five
   b)   411
   c)   98°
   d)   Blink-182

2.   This group of guys (J, Scott, Abs, Ritchie, and Sean) comes from Europe, where their song "When the Lights Go Out" was a smash hit.

   a)   Five
   b)   3 Doors Down
   c)   Sixpence None the Richer
   d)   2gether

QUIZ 7

3. These three friends — Irish, LeMisha, and Kameelah — named their band after their Las Vegas area code.

a) 311
b) Blink-182
c) 702
d) SK8

4. This band's lead singer, Rob Thomas, teamed up with Carlos Santana on the Grammy-winning smash hit "Smooth."

a) 98°
b) Five
c) Take 5
d) matchbox twenty

5. This Norwegian girl duo's song "Don't Say You Love Me" can be heard on the *Pokémon: The First Movie* soundtrack.

a) 702
b) 311
c) M2M
d) S Club 7

6. This girl band's name is short for the title of a famous book by Louisa May Alcott, and it's not *Little Men*!

a) Sister2Sister
b) 3LW
c) Eve 6
d) 311

7. "Poor" Leigh, Matt, Dale, Justin, and Sean—their top song was on the *She's All That* soundtrack!

a) Sixpence None the Richer
b) Eve 6
c) Five
d) S Club 7

8. Even if you blink you won't miss all the tattoos on this band's drummer, Travis Barker. He claims to have between forty and fifty!

a) Blink-182
b) Five
c) 3 Doors Down
d) matchbox twenty

QUIZ 7

9. The lead singer of this band wanted to be an environmental lawyer! But he decided that music was a better way to spend his "Semi-Charmed Life."
a) Third Eye Blind
b) 504 Boyz
c) 311
d) Blink-182

10. This band toured with LFO and put singer Brad Fischetti in a 3-D video!
a) S Club 7
b) M2M
c) SK8
d) Sister2Sister

11. This close-knit boy band made their debut in a movie created just for MTV.
a) 98°
b) 702
c) Sister Seven
d) 2gether

12. These rappers made a hit with their song "Wobble, Wobble." Hint: There are not a lotta girlz here.

a) 98°
b) Five
c) 504 Boyz
d) Sister2Sister

13. This Europop group gets their name from a famous, tall landmark in France called the Eiffel Tower.

a) matchbox twenty
b) S Club 7
c) Eiffel 65
d) Sixpence None the Richer

14. This boy and girl group has been compared to The Jackson Five because of the way they harmonize.

a) S Club 7
b) 311
c) Eve 6
d) Five

QUIZ 7

15. This band's hit song "Absolutely (Story of a Girl)" was played nonstop on radio stations in summer 2000!

a)   matchbox twenty
b)   KRS-One
c)   98°
d)   Nine Days

Scorecard

1–5 right: Count you out of this pop quiz!
Pop Points: 0
6–10 right: This score just *barely* adds up!
Pop Points: 1
11–14 right: Way to go! You've done a number on this quiz! **Pop Points: 3**
All 15 right: You get BIG bonus points in the numbers category! **Pop Points: 10**

Pop Point Total _____

PARTY GAME
Lotsa Laughs

Lighten up! Even if you didn't get a perfect point spread in the last numbers game, you can make up for it with Lotsa Laughs. First, have everyone sit down in a circle. Then one person starts the game by saying "Ha." The next person says, "Ha, ha," and so on around the circle. The catch: You can't really laugh. How long will you last? Last person left *not* laughing is the winner.

The winner earns five bonus Pop Points!

¿QUIZ 8

Quirks

Your favorite pop stars have some funny favorites and some even funnier habits. How quickly can you answer these quirky questions?

1. A.J. from the Backstreet Boys has what kind of cuddly pet?
a) Iguanas
b) Two shih tzus
c) Twelve frogs

2. Gwen Stefani from No Doubt thinks this snack takes the cake.
a) Beef jerky
b) Pea soup
c) Chocolate

? ? ? Celebrity Quiz-o-rama™ ? ? ?

3.   Freddie Prinze, Jr., is known for doing this all the time on sets.

a) Eating too many jelly doughnuts

b) Jumping up and down on ~~one~~ foot

c) Playing practical jokes on his costars

4.   Kerr Smith from *Dawson's Creek* calls himself a nerd . . . why?

a) He loves playing on the computer.

b) He wears a tie all the time.

c) He's never left his house.

5.   In order to keep her midriff in shape, Britney Spears does what every morning?

a) ~~One~~ hundred sit-ups

b) ~~One~~ thousand belly-dancing shakes

c) ~~Five~~ hundred handstands

6.   What band's member Rich Cronin has been known to use toothpaste as hair gel?

a) 'N Sync

b) No Authority

c) LFO

QUIZ 8

7. What Canadian band has triplets in it?

a) Boyzone
b) The Moffatts
c) ~~Five~~

8. What '70s band's songs does the Swedish group A*Teens sing?

a) The Bee Gees
b) ABBA
c) The Pointer Sisters

9. Why was heartthrob Leonardo DiCaprio rejected from his first audition?

a) Bad hair day
b) He had a big zit on his nose.
c) He arrived ~~three~~ hours late.

10. Before livin' *la vida loca*, **who appeared on the soap opera** *General Hospital* **as a Latin singing star?**

a) Ricky Martin
b) Marc Anthony
c) Enrique Iglesias

? ? ? Celebrity Quiz-o-rama™ ? ? ?

11. What food do the members of 'N Sync need backstage at their concerts?

a) Cold ~~fish~~ sticks
b) Creamed spinach
c) Pop Tarts

12. Whose hot music video did _Saved by the Bell_'s "Screech" appear in?

a) 98°
b) 'N Sync
c) Christina Aguilera

Scorecard

1–4 right: OK, so trivia isn't your thing!
Pop Points: Nada
5–8 right: Quirks work for you — a little bit.
Pop Points: 1
9–11 right: How weird — you got so many answers right! **Pop Points: 2**
All 12 right: YESSSSSSSS! **Pop Points: 3**

Pop Point Total _____

?UIZ 9

Alphabet Soup

There are so many bands and singers with letters in their name! Can you answer nineteen true or false questions about these B-A-N-D-S?

1. LFO stands for Lyte Fantastic Ones.

2. LL Cool J got his name from a friend who said the ladies loved "cool" James.

3. TLC got their name because they are all about Tender Loving Care!

4. M2M is a boy band.

5. KRS-One is a country music superstar.

6. Each member of R Angels auditioned for her spot in the group.

7. Vitamin C sings a song about graduation.

8. Nick Carter is a member of 'N Sync.

9. PYT stands for Pretty Young Things.

10. Singer Q-Tip got his name because he uses a lot of cotton swabs.

? ? ? Celebrity Quiz-o-rama™ ? ? ?

11. R.E.M. sings the song "Bye Bye Bye."

12. The * in B*witched stands for the letter "E."

13. Bond is the lead singer of the group U2.

14. There are four members of BSB.

15. KRS-One stands for Knowledge Reigns Supreme over Nearly Everyone.

16. The Latin group with the debut album "Different Kind of Love" is T-Note.

17. British group S Club 7 has a TV show called *S Club 7 in Miami*.

18. Naturi, Kiely, and Adrienne make up the trio called 3W.

19. Lead singer Dave Matthews leads the popular group DMB.

Scorecard

1–8 right: You get an O, for Oopsie! **Pop Points: -1**

9–14 right: E for effort, see? **Pop Points: 1**

15–18 right: B+ makes the grade! **Pop Points: 4**

All 19 right: Wow! Letter perfect deserves LOTS of points. **Pop Points: 10**

Pop Point Total _____

PARTY GAME
Pop Goes the Letter

The goal of this game is to use up the letters of the alphabet as creatively as possible — as quickly as possible!

Start out by picking a subject that describes a setting (like record store) or an event (like getting out of ~~school~~ for the summer).

Next, select a letter as a starting point. You don't have to start with A. For example, start with P.

The first person to talk uses that letter to start a discussion on the chosen subject. For example, if you picked "getting out of ~~school~~ for the summer" and then chose the letter P, you could start out by saying "Please let me out of ~~school~~!"

The next person continues the game by moving to the next letter of the alphabet and saying something different about the subject. For example, in this game, the next person could say "Quiet! I'm studying for my last test," and the person after that could say, "Ready for camp, every~~one~~?" and so on. You go from P to Q, R, and the rest. It continues on like this until you work your way through the whole alphabet.

Here's the important part of the game: Keeping it moving! The key to playing this is making it FAST. It can get pretty silly, especially if you only have twenty seconds to think of a response!

Consider using pop star themes for the game, too. Take all your responses into a theme like "all about the show *Popular*" or "all about Backstreet Boys." Have fun!

Give yourself a Pop Point for playing!

Pop Point Total _____

ŞUIZ 10

Karaoke Club

Believe it or not, pop stars of all kinds have songs in *their* hearts, too. What if Nick Carter and his l'il brother Aaron got up to do a duet . . . what song would they choose? Lots of stars have given a big shout out about the songs they love — and would sing at a karaoke club. . . .

1.   This singer, nicknamed "Dragon," says he would sing anything by Janet Jackson or Erykah Badu.
   a)   Crisco
   b)   Disco
   c)   Sisqó

2.   Nick Lachey and Jessica Simpson would probably sing this, their own duet.
   a)   "Where You Are"
   b)   "Leave Me Alone"
   c)   "Get Off My Back"

? ? ? Celebrity Quiz-o-rama™ ? ? ?

3.   *10 Things I Hate About You*'s Larisa Oleynik loooooooves this girl band.
a)   Cleopatra
b)   Veruca Salt
c)   LFO

4.   *Roswell* hunk Jason Behr thinks this classic "bug" band is tops.
a)   The Butterflies
b)   The Caterpillars
c)   The Beatles

5.   MTV's Carson Daly says he likes listening and singing along with this band's superhit "All the Small Things."
a)   98°
b)   Blink-182
c)   BB Mak

6.   Drew Barrymore grooves to songs by her pal Courtney Love's band.
a)   Pile
b)   Hole
c)   Ditch

7. **You'll find these classic blues singers on Will Smith's favorite CDs. He loves to lip-synch with them!**

a) Stevie Wonder and Aretha Franklin

b) Raffi and Wee Sing

c) Britney Spears and Christina Aguilera

8. **Melissa Joan Hart will be singin' in honor of her own movie, *Drive Me Crazy*. She loves this Britney Spears tune most of all.**

a) "Crazy for You"

b) "(You Drive Me) Crazy"

c) "Let's Go Crazy"

9. **Since he got nominated for an Oscar for the movie *Sixth Sense*, it seems right that Haley Joel Osment loves singing this song.**

a) Christina Aguilera's "What a Girl Wants"

b) 'N Sync's "Tearin' Up My Heart"

c) Smash Mouth's "All Star"

? ? ? Celebrity Quiz-o-rama™ ? ? ?

10. This cool cutie loves his big brother's band, Backstreet Boys, and their mega-hit "As Long As You Love Me."

a) Aaron Carter
b) Zac Hanson
c) Rich Cronin

Scorecard

1–3 right: Your lip-synch . . . *sunk*. **Pop Points: -1**

4–6 right: You're *half*-wrong about the songs. **Pop Points: 0**

7–9 right: Sing out about *this* close-to-perfect score! **Pop Points: 1**

All 10 right: The crown is yours. **Pop Points: 3**

Pop Point Total _____

PARTY GAME
Singalong

Part One

Let's see some identification . . . please! Pull out your favorite CDs and MP3s and start namin' names — and songs. How many songs and singers can your party guests ID just from hearing a few lines of lyrics? Here's the fun part: You don't sing the lyrics, you *say* 'em. It makes it tougher to guess.

Or play three seconds of a song and see if your guests can name the song.

~~One~~ other idea is to call out common words like "love," "heart," and "feel." Then give everyone at the party ~~five~~ minutes to write down all the songs they can think of containing those words.

Part Two

Transform your living room into a music studio . . . where YOU are the star. Pop on your favorite CDs, click on the radio, turn to MTV, or whatever it takes to get the music ON! Using a

? ? ? Celebrity Quiz-o-rama™ ? ? ?

hairbrush, Magic Marker, or some kind of microphone stand-in . . . sing out!

Take turns doing "at home" karaoke or lip-synching, and see which pop party guest gets all the notes right!

Give yourself a Pop Point for playing!

Pop Point Total _____

¿UIZ 11
Family Affair

There are a lot of close relations in the music and movie world. Can you make these connections work?

1. One brother stars in big-screen movies while the other has appeared more on the small screen . . . on several seasons of *Party of Five*.
a) Drew and Nick Lachey
b) Neve and Christian Campbell
c) Jeremy and Jason London

2. These animated siblings fight crime before bedtime!
a) Lisa, Bart, and Maggie Simpson
b) The Powerpuff Girls Blossom, Buttercup and Bubbles
c) The X-Men

55

? ? ? Celebrity Quiz-o-rama™ ? ? ?

3. *That '70s Show* star, Danny Masterson, has a younger brother, Christopher Kennedy Masterson, who plays Francis in which popular TV show?

a) *Popular*
b) *Roswell*
c) *Malcolm in the Middle*

4. These Canadian brothers are definitely not singing the blues.

a) The Moffatts
b) The Muppets
c) The Mopheads

5. If you took the temperature of these two band brothers, it would come out to be a perfect ninety-eight degrees.

a) Jeremy and Jason London
b) Nick and Aaron Carter
c) Drew and Nick Lachey

6. Jessica Simpson's sister works with her when she performs. What does Ashley do?

a) She loads and unloads the trucks.
b) She is one of her dancers.
c) She passes out programs at shows.

7. These ~~two~~ actor brothers from Massachusetts ended up in Hollywood. One even has an Academy Award!

    a)   Matt and Gabriel Damon
    b)   Jeremy and Jason London
    c)   Casey and Ben Affleck

8. These ~~two~~ sisters work closely together, even if they're not on the same show! ~~One~~ plays a character on live action TV, while the other is a voice for a cartoon character!

    a)   Melissa Joan Hart and her little sister Emily
    b)   Brittany and Cynthia Daniel
    c)   Mary-Kate and Ashley Olsen

9. ~~One~~ movie star brother was left *Home Alone* while the other brother got a lift from *The Mighty*.

    a)   Ben and Fred Savage
    b)   Macaulay and Kieran Culkin
    c)   Ben and Casey Affleck

10. Fred Savage starred on the old show *The Wonder Years* when he was a kid, while his brother Ben starred on what TGIF show?

a) *Boy Meets World*
b) *The Wonder Years II*
c) *Freaks and Geeks*

11. Ray Norwood has a famous sister who recorded a hit song with pop star Monica. Now Ray costars on his sister's TV show. Who's his super sis?

a) Aaliyah
b) Pink
c) Brandy

12. Mmm! What Tulsa, Oklahoma, brothers recorded a bopping tune that made them a relative sensation?

a) Tyrese
b) Third Eye Blind
c) Hanson

13. Twins Edele and Keavy Lynch are members of what pop group?

a) B*witched
b) Innosense
c) R Angels

QUIZ 11

14. ~~One~~ BSB made *People* magazine's hot list just as his younger brother started his own cool crooning career.
  a) Drew and Nick Lachey
  b) Nick and Aaron Carter
  c) Jeremy and Jason London

15. Her brother Kris is an actor who's just starting his career, but Carly Pope is the ~~one~~ in a network series. What is it?
  a) *Young Americans*
  b) *Roswell*
  c) *Popular*

16. These smiling sibs started out on *Full House* and now they make movies, videos, and more.
  a) Tia and Tamera Mowry
  b) Candace and Kirk Cameron
  c) Mary-Kate and Ashley Olsen

17. Both of the Spelling siblings appeared on this '90s TV show. Tori was a regular and Randy was a guest star.
  a) *Sunset Beach*
  b) *Beverly Hills, 90210*
  c) *Dawson's Creek*

? ? ? Celebrity Quiz-o-rama™ ? ? ?

Scorecard

1-6 right: You've got so-so sibling sense!
Pop Points: 2
7-12 right: The family ~~tree~~'s still missin' a few branches. **Pop Points: 4**
13-16 right: You know your family history!
Pop Points: 6
All 17 right: WOW! Who put you in charge of this family reunion? **Pop Points: 8**

Pop Point Total _____

PARTY GAME
Pop Star Twist

Ready to twist and shout about the cutie-patootie pop stars you adore? Everybody . . . TWIST!

Before you can play, you'll need to make the twister board on the floor.

1. Write names of the stars you oogle on pieces of 8 1/2″ x 11″ paper. That's the same size paper that's in your notebook. Write 'em big in marker so you can read them when they're down on the floor . . . OR . . . rip out single pages from magazines you love — featuring full-color faces of the same stars.

2. Take the pictures or name sheets and tape them together like a quilt. You should have five rows of four, or twenty squares total. Place this on the floor.

3. On another single sheet of paper, write those twenty names in small boxes so that you can cut them up and toss into a hat.

4. Have one person in charge of reading the "destination" squares. This person is the emcee. Everyone else is going to twist.

5. The emcee pulls a name from the hat, reads it aloud, and tosses the name back in.

6. When the name is read, the "twister" puts ~~one~~ hand or foot on that square. Then the emcee reads another name out loud. The next "twister" puts his or her hand or foot on *that* square. Because you toss the star's name back into the hat, more than ~~one~~ "twister's" hand or foot could end up on each square.

7. The emcee continues to read out names until everyone is twisted into a knot on the floor. Funny!

8. Whoever stays upright the longest . . . WINS. **Give yourself a Pop Point for playing!**

QUIZ 12
Charity Case

Superstars like to give generously of their time and money. How cool! Below are fifteen charitable clues to who gives where. How many star names can you unscramble?

1. This *7th Heaven* sweetheart formed her own charity called Grand Prix Kids to help underprivileged kids.

YBLEVERE   LIMTHECL

_____   _____

2. These four singing brothers from Canada are majorly involved in the Make-A-Wish Foundation.

ETH   TAFMSOTF

____   _____

? ? ? Celebrity Quiz-o-rama™ ? ? ?

3. This not-so-*Clueless* (the movie) superstar is super-involved in animal rights organizations.

IAILAC   OVELRISENST

_____   _____

4. Nobody forced this singing sensation to take any jagged little pills in order to support the human rights organization Amnesty International.

NSLAIA   RIOTMSESET

_____   _____

5. This hunk interviewed President Clinton in his role as the Chairman of Earth Day 2000.

AODLNREO   CIOIDRPA

_____   _____

6. No "oops!" here. She started a summer camp for underprivileged kids who wanna sing and dance.

YEBTRNI   RAPSSE

_____   _____

7. From *Star Wars* to star causes, this actress speaks out for pediatric AIDS.

TLIENAA   RPMTONA

_____   _____

QUIZ 12

8. Taking a breath of clean air is a lot more than "Fantasy" to this chart-topping diva from New York. She supports the Fresh Air Fund.

AMHRAI   YERCA

_____   _____

9. This band goes ga ga over feeding the hungry with USA Harvest.

OGO   OOG   LOSOD

_____   _____   _____

10. This ex-Fugee is definitely not mis-educated about her incredible camp for kids.

NUYLAR   LHLI

_____   _____

11. When he had emergency surgery on his own heart, this BSB member started campaigning for pediatric cardiology.

RIANB   TLLLREIT

_____   _____

12. When this boy meets world, he says "don't smoke!" He supports the Campaign for Tobacco-Free Kids.

BNE   AEGVAS

_____   _____

Scorecard

1–4 right: Something's gotta give! **Pop Points: -1**

5–8 right: You generously answered half correctly. **Pop Points: 1**

9–11 right: You give charitable stars a good name! **Pop Points: 3**

All 12 right: There are plenty of right answers to go around! **Pop Points: 5**

Pop Point Total _____

?UIZ 13

For Sale

Sometimes we see stars we like selling stuff in magazines or on TV. How many can you identify? Good luck!

1.   She's posed in ads for everything from Sony Psyc Portable Music players to Blue Asphalt Blue Jeans to Neutrogena! But no candy . . . yet!
a)   Jessica Simpson
b)   Britney Spears
c)   Mandy Moore

2.   Her face — and feet — can be seen in Candies ads . . . that are just Charmed!
a)   Hoku
b)   Alyssa Milano
c)   Melissa Joan Hart

? ? ? Celebrity Quiz-o-rama™ ? ? ?

3. This hunky singer shines like two thousand watts when he poses in ads for Guess jeans.
a) Aaron Carter
b) Shane Filan
c) Tyrese

4. Clothing designer Tommy Hilfiger found out that this singer could sell jeans and music, baby . . . one more time!
a) Christina Aguilera
b) Britney Spears
c) Mandy Moore

5. She's giving a little TLC in her ads for Calvin Klein jeans.
a) Lisa "Left Eye" Lopes
b) Aaliyah
c) Jessica Simpson

6. Catch her on *Moesha* . . . or in ads for DKNY jeans.
a) Melissa Joan Hart
b) Brandy
c) Hoku

QUIZ 13

7. This former *Party of Five* regular smiles back at you from Neutrogena ads in magazines and on television.

a) Lacey Chabert
b) Neve Campbell
c) Jennifer Love Hewitt

8. This super-cast of a television show all appeared in ads for Levi's in a special 2000 campaign.

a) *Freaks and Geeks*
b) *Roswell*
c) *Dawson's Creek*

9. She's a slayer in ads for Maybelline.

a) Sarah Michelle Gellar
b) Jennifer Love Hewitt
c) Britney Spears

10. Her shocking hair color earned her the right to pose in cool ads for Jelly Roll colored pens.

a) Macy Gray
b) Pink
c) Gwen Stefani

? ? ? Celebrity Quiz-o-rama™ ? ? ?

11. She's got a white smile and strong, healthy bones. Is that why "Got Milk?" chose this singing sensation to pose for them twice . . . and sponsored her summer 2000 tour?

a) Britney Spears
b) Christina Aguilera
c) Jessica Simpson

12. She's got the natural look covered in her ads for Cover Girl.

a) Hoku
b) Mandy Moore
c) Brandy

Scorecard

1–4 right: You're a stylin' wannabe. **Pop Points: -1**
5–8 right: You look *okay*. **Pop Points: 1**
9–11 right: You're lookin' *real* good. **Pop Points: 3**
All 12 right: You have got the look — and the POINTS! **Pop Points: 6**

Pop Point Total _____

PARTY GAME
Beauty Shoppe: Just for Girls

Have a spa in the middle of your living room. You and your friends can get beautiful *together*!

Here are some ideas for how you can pamper yourself and have fun at the same time.

Get a jar of facial mask (ask Mom to help you). It will be fun to sit around and wait for the masks to be peelable!

Get lots of funny makeup so you can give each other wild makeovers.

Have barrettes, elastics, scrunchies, and ribbons on hand so you can do major 'dos!

Manicure? Sure! Your friends will love getting their nails painted. You can gossip about your favorite TV, music, and movie stars.

The *best* kind of makeover? POP STAR! You and your friends can make yourselves over like Britney, Christina, Mandy, and anyone else! Try on different clothes, makeup, and don't forget to dance around the room!

Give yourself a Pop Point for playing!

Pop Point Total ____

₂UIZ 14
O'er the Rainbow

Do pop bands come in all sorts of colors? You bet! The pop scene is a rainbow just waiting to be discovered. Below are ten statements about colorful bands. Are they true . . . or false?

1. The **Indigo** Girls are a new wave polka band.

2. **Pink**'s hit song "There You Go" got her lots of attention.

3. Macy **Gray** was nominated for a Grammy Award, but she lost to Christina Aguilera.

4. The band **Aqua** had a smash hit with the song "Baby Girl."

5. The lead singer of the band **Silver**chair is Bart Simpson.

6. **Green** Day has three members.

7. Some members of **Blaque** used to be in another band called Butz.

QUIZ 14

8. The lead singer of **Blue**s Traveler wears a special accordion vest onstage.

Scorecard

1–3 right: You got the blues. **Pop Points: 0**
4–5 right: Shades of gray. **Pop Points: 1**
6–7 right: The white stuff. **Pop Points: 3**
All 8 right: Coloriffic! **Pop Points: 6**

Pop Point Total _____

¿UIZ 15
Also Known As

For the final quiz of the party, see how well your friends can identify the *real* names of stars. First, a full list of names you'd find on that star's birth certificate. Then, a list of stage names that we know and see all the time. Can you match up all 26 sets of names?

1. Jennifer Anistonapoulos
2. Marco Antonio Muniz
3. Mark Andrews
4. Brian Ray Ulrich
5. Aaliyah Haughton
6. Tara Patrick
7. Jennifer Mary Butala
8. Dana Ellane Owens
9. Gloria Maria Fajardo
10. Alecia Moore
11. Courtney Harrison

a) Sisqó
b) Demi Moore
c) Jennifer Aniston
d) Sting
e) Carmen Electra
f) Queen Latifah
g) Pink
h) Usher
i) Aaliyah
j) Marc Anthony
k) Skeet Ulrich

QUIZ 15

12. Colleen Fitzpatrick
13. Tionne Watkins
14. Jonathan Davis Kamal IV
15. Demetria Guynes
16. Julie Roberts
17. Eileen Regina Edwards
18. Usher Raymond IV
19. Eldrick Woods
20. Artis Ivey Jr.
21. Shawntae Harris
22. Rozonda Thomas
23. Lisa Lopes
24. Gordon Matthew Sumner
25. Sean Combs
26. Jewel Kilcher

l) Julia Roberts
m) Jenna Elfman
n) Q-Tip
o) Left Eye
p) Jewel
q) Shania Twain
r) Da Brat
s) Puff Daddy
t) Tiger Woods
u) Vitamin C
v) Coolio
w) Courtney Love
x) Gloria Estefan
y) Chili
z) T-Boz

Scorecard

1–10 right: **Pop Points: 5**
11–17 right: **Pop Points: 15**
20–25 right: **Pop Points: 25**
All 26 right: Try *this* name on for size:
POP PERFECTION!: 35

Pop Point Total _____

PARTY GAMES
Pop Star Showcase

This last game is a lot of fun to play, especially after having been through all this great pop trivia!

Send one player out of the room.

While he/she is gone, the rest of the group decides on a pop star. When the absent person returns, he/she will have to guess the name of the star. The clues will need to be acted out silently by all the players.

Maybe the star chosen is Christina Aguilera. When the person returns to the room, he/she then asks the other players to do something like the pop star would do. For example, the person trying to guess would ask the group, "Please dance like the pop star," and they would. Or the person might ask, "Please act out a scene from the pop star's top video." Then the group would have to act it out.

If the chosen star is an actor or actress, the person guessing can ask the group to silently act out part of the star's most famous movie. All questions and actions are performed like a "pop star showcase" just as the star would do it on stage or on the big screen.

You can also play this game with no actions — only descriptions. For example, if the mystery pop star was still Christina, the person guessing could ask the group to describe what the star looks like or to sing some of the star's lyrics. If the star is an actor or actress, the person guessing could ask what awards they've won, or if the star does TV and/or movies.

It's a great way to showcase your new pop star expertise!

Give yourself a Pop Point for playing!

Pop Point Total _____

? ? ? Celebrity Quiz-o-rama™ ? ? ?

POP POINT SCORECARD

Before you tally up your final score, check out page 81 for the answers to the questions on the photo pages and on the back cover of this book.

Give yourself five bonus Pop Points if you answered at least eight of these questions correctly.

You made it through all the games and quizzes! Way to go! Now it's time to go back, count up your Pop Points, and see how you rate.

POP POINT TOTAL   POP RATING

0–20   TOO POOPED TO POP

Looks like you've fallen out of the pop loop! You wouldn't know a member of the Backstreet Boys if one walked up to you on the street and said HEL-LO! But that's OK. With a little practice, you, too, could be *pop*-tacular. Try reading magazines and checking out the new music videos every now and then. Maybe the party's Pop Prince/Princess could even give you a few pointers.

? ? ? Celebrity Quiz-o-rama™ ? ? ?

21–60   **POP AMATEUR**

Okay. You know some pop stuff, but the truth is that you don't know the difference between Britney and Christina . . . *yet*. There's hope, though! Tune into your favorite TV shows, grab some 'zines, and feel the pop flow. You won't be an amateur for much longer. That's a pop promise!

61–100   **POP PRO**

Here's the pop story with you: You like a little pop stargazing, but you're not one hundred percent in the know. Chances are that, from across a crowded room, you'd definitely recognize Frankie Muniz from *Malcolm in the Middle*, but you'd be less sure about putting a "Hello, My Name Is . . . " label on Alanis Morissette's jacket. Not to worry! With a little practice, you will be pop *perfect*.

101–146   **TOP OF THE POPS**

How do things look from the top of the pop ladder? Pretty cool up here, huh? You have scaled a mountain of pop questions and reached the peak in no time flat! Howd'ja do it? Have you been poppin' around magazine stands for the latest issues of *Twist* and *Teen*?

? ? ? Celebrity Quiz-o-rama™ ? ? ?

Where do you go from here? Believe it or not, you can still aspire to be . . .

147–infinity   MOST POP-ULAR

You got so many points they could barely be counted. You have reached the pinnacle of pop. Well, for this book at least. You know obscure pop stars and super celebs alike! You even got most of the games right! Did you ever guess you'd get so many bonus Pop Points? You did! Watch out though . . . if you're not careful, the "pop"parazzi will start hounding you for photos and an autograph!

DON'T FORGET!

Whoever gets the most Pop Points at the party should immediately be crowned . . . POP PRINCE / PRINCESS! Congratulations to everyone who played! Now, get to bed, sleepyheads! Unless, of course, you want to stay up all night talking.

ANSWER KEY

Back Cover Answers: Christina is older than Britney — but not by much. Christina was born on December 18, 1980, and Britney was born on December 2, 1981; A.J. stands for Alexander James; David Boreanaz stars in the TV show *Angel*; Tangi Miller is on *Felicity*.

Photo Quiz Answers: Britney's middle name is Jean; Lance Bass appeared on *Who Wants to Be a Millionaire*; James Marsden starred in *X-Men*; Jennifer Love Hewitt's friends call her Love; Frankie Muniz stars in *Malcom in the Middle*; Freddie Prinze, Jr. is really good friends with Sarah Michelle Gellar; False, BSK did not win a Grammy for "I Want it That Way"; Leslie Bibb and Carly Pope star on *Popular*; True, in real life Ashton Kutcher does have a twin brother; Jason Behr was born in Minnesota; Christina is older than Britney.

Quiz 1 Answers: 1c, 2b, 3c, 4a, 5b, 6b, 7a, 8a, 9b, 10c, 11b, 12c, 13a, 14b, 15c

? ? ? Celebrity Quiz-o-rama™ ? ? ?

Quiz 2 Answers: 1c, 2d, 3b, 4d, 5a, 6d, 7b, 8c, 9b, 10b, 11d, 12a

Quiz 3 Answers:
1. *Austin Powers*
2. *Men in Black*
3. Sarah Michelle Gellar
4. *Titanic*
5. *Malcolm in the Middle*
6. *Stuart Little*
7. Natalie Portman
8. *Ever After*
9. Ben Savage
10. *The Simpsons*
11. *Popular*
12. Joshua Jackson
13. Shiri Appleby
14. *Sabrina, the Teenage Witch*
15. Heath Ledger
16. *Friends*

Quiz 4 Answers: 1b, 2c, 3b, 4b, 5a, 6d, 7b, 8d, 9a, 10a, 11b, 12c

Bonus Answer: *Winona* Ryder, of course!

ANSWER KEY

Quiz 5 Answers: 1b, 2c, 3a, 4d, 5d, 6c, 7b, 8b, 9d, 10a, 11b, 12c, 13d, 14a, 15b, 16a, 17b, 18c

Quiz 6 Answers:
1. Sugar Ray
2. The Lox
3. Fiona Apple
4. Meatloaf
5. Salt-n-Pepa
6. The Cranberries
7. Spice Girls
8. Lemonheads
9. Brandy
10. Blowfish
11. Smashing Pumpkins

Bonus Answer: Vitamin C

Quiz 7 Answers: 1c, 2a, 3c, 4d, 5c, 6b (3 *Little Women*), 7a, 8a, 9a, 10c, 11d, 12c, 13c, 14a, 15d

Quiz 8 Answers: 1b, 2c, 3c, 4a, 5a, 6c, 7b, 8b, 9a, 10a, 11c, 12a

? ? ? Celebrity Quiz-o-rama™ ? ? ?

Quiz 9 Answers:

1. False. It doesn't stand for anything! It used to be Lyte *Funky* Ones, but not anymore.

2. True.

3. False. TLC are the first initials in each of the band member's names: T-Boz, Left Eye, and Chili.

4. False. M2M is a two-girl duet.

5. False. KRS-One is a rapper.

6. True.

7. True.

8. False. Nick Carter is in the Backstreet Boys.

9. True.

10. False. He got the name Q-Tip because his hair poofs up like a white Q-Tip on top of his head.

11. False. 'N Sync sings that song.

12. True.

13. False. The lead singer of U2 is Bono. There is no one named Bond in U2!

14. False! There are *five* members of BSB, or Backstreet Boys.

15. True.

16. False. The group is C-Note.

17. True.

18. False. The group's name is 3LW, for 3 Little Women.

ANSWER KEY

19. True. DMB stands for the Dave Matthews Band, as a matter of fact!

Quiz 10 Answers: 1c, 2a, 3b, 4c, 5b, 6b, 7a, 8b, 9c, 10a

Quiz 11 Answers: 1c, 2b, 3c, 4a, 5c, 6b, 7c, 8a, 9b, 10a, 11c, 12c, 13a, 14b, 15c, 16c, 17b

Quiz 12 Answers:
1. Beverley Mitchell
2. The Moffatts
3. Alicia Silverstone
4. Alanis Morissette
5. Leonardo DiCaprio
6. Britney Spears
7. Natalie Portman
8. Mariah Carey
9. Goo Goo Dolls
10. Lauryn Hill
11. Brian Littrell
12. Ben Savage

Quiz 13 Answers: 1c, 2b, 3c, 4b, 5a, 6b, 7c, 8b, 9a, 10b, 11a, 12c

? ? ? Celebrity Quiz-o-rama™ ? ? ?

Quiz 14 Answers: 1. False. The Indigo Girls are a rock and folk duet. 2. True. 3. True. 4. False. The hit song was "Barbie Girl." 5. False. Silverchair's lead singer is named Daniel Johns. You know who Bart Simpson is, right? 6. True. 7. True 8. False. He wears a *harmonica* vest. What would an accordion vest look like?

Quiz 15 Answers:

1. c	7. m	13. z	19. t	25. s
2. j	8. f	14. n	20. v	26. p
3. a	9. x	15. b	21. r	
4. k	10. g	16. l	22. y	
5. i	11. w	17. q	23. o	
6. e	12. u	18. h	24. d	

Can't get enough of your favorite rock, pop, R & B, and Hip-Hop stars?

Check out
Celebrity Quiz-o-rama #2:
MUSIC MANIA!

❓ **Break this code to find out Aaliyah's real name: LLWTJLS**

❓ **98° plus A*Teen plus TLC = how many people?**

Strut your stuff with crosswords, secret codes, word searches, brain-teasers, and more all about your favorite music makers and shakers. Rack up Pop Points along the way to find the chart topper among all your friends!

POP TO IT!